NORTH OF IRELAND

FOLK TALES FOR CHILDREN

DOREEN MCBRIDE

The History Press

*This book is dedicated to the pupils,
and teachers, of Edenderry Primary School,
Banbridge, who encouraged me in my
wickedness and made helpful comments.*

Illustrated by the author.
Cover illustration by Su Eaton

WARNING: This book is
not suitable for adults.

First published 2019

The History Press
The Mill, Brimscombe Port
Stroud, Gloucestershire, GL5 2QG
www.thehistorypress.co.uk

British Library Cataloguing in Publication Data.
A catalogue record for this book is available from the British Library.

ISBN 978 0 7509 8800 1

Typesetting and origination by The History Press
Printed in Great Britain

CONTENTS

FOREWORD

Do you know what folk tales are? I think they're the kind of stories that have been handed down from the past. I think they mention real people and real events that have been exaggerated and changed over time so they're unrecognisable. For instance, we know from historical records there once was a king Brian Boru, but I don't believe his toes talked to each other! Do you? I also think there was a king called Conor and that an Irishman, called Conall Cearnach, was present at the Crucifixion. But did King Conor have a heart attack and die when he was told about it? Who knows?

My Granny Henry told me folk stories and I haven't stopped telling them since! When I was young I told stories to my teddy bear and anything, or anyone, else who'd listen. After I had trained as a teacher I used to love scaring my pupils by telling them terrible tales, especially before lunch time. Then about thirty years ago I became a professional storyteller.

It was fun. I travelled the world on my tongue. It was like being paid to go on holiday. All I had to do was talk too much, and I do that anyway. Then I thought, 'When I die my stories will die too!' so I started to write them down.

This book contains some of my favourites. I hope you enjoy them, too. They are full of naughty words like piddle and poo, knickers and bum because people in folk tales must have had to piddle and poo, although not all of them wore knickers but they all had bums and did wee smelly ones and big smelly ones! In other words, they were human like you and me.

INTRODUCTION

I t gives me great pleasure to introduce Doreen McBride's new book of folk tales from the North of Ireland for children.

Doreen is a member of that ancient Irish profession – the seanachies or professional storytellers. I first met Doreen some thirty years ago on a dark, crisp Hallowe'en night. She sat in the ingle of a crackling turf fire, in an old-fashioned Irish cottage on the County Down coast. A born storyteller, she had gathered round her a rapt audience of children who hung on her every word as she transported them (and their parents) back to the lost world of Ireland long ago with tales of Tir-na-nOg ('The Land of the Ever Young'), the Fairy Thorn and the Banshee. On that special night when tradition claims that ghosts and goblins stalk the land, Doreen enraptured her audience, who lingered long after the last tale was told, fearful of the long walk back down the dark Loanin and past the graveyard beyond.

In this book, Doreen McBride offers a medley of folk tales, old and new. The young reader will encounter King Brian Boru, the man who defeated the fierce Vikings and died at the Battle of Clontarf in 1014, as he grapples with a more challenging emergency. They will meet Bricu 'of the bitter tongue' (after whom Loughbrickland in County Down takes its name). They will travel with our esteemed storyteller to Cuchulain's country in County Louth, where they will hear a scintillating tale about the ancient dolmen at Proleek – a kind of warrior's tomb, enshrouded in mystery.

Here too we find the age-old story of how Robert the Bruce, King of Scotland, sought refuge in a cave on Rathlin Island, off the North Antrim coast, and was inspired by the determination of a spider there to return and save his native land. There are stirring tales of Finn McCool and the legend of the Giant's Causeway – now a world-class heritage site. The traditional story of St Patrick and how he built first the church at Saul, Co. Down (from the Irish Sabhal, a barn) is beautifully told.

For me, however, the selection of ghost stories at the end of this volume evoked memories of spine-chilling tales of my childhood long ago. Read Doreen's tales of the ghostly highwayman of Cave Hill (the swash-buckling Belfast 'rapparee', Naoise O'Haughan, executed at Carrickfergus Jail in 1720), the Ghost of Belfast's historic harbour office and the tragic 'spectres' of the Lucifer match factory fire and sleep if you can!

Doreen McBride has used her legendary story-telling skills and imagination to create a series of thrilling, locally based folk tales that combine a sense of the past with a blend of mystery, suspense and excitement.

This book will be enjoyed by a host of eager young readers.

Dr Éamon Phoenix
Historian and Broadcaster

1

KING BRIAN BORU'S TALKING TOES

D o you sleep with your socks on? If so, it's a sure sign that you're descended from King Brian Boru, the High King of Ireland. He had, as you can imagine, a very stressful, tiring job.

One morning King Brian Boru was so tired he could hardly get out of bed, so he turned to his wife and said, 'Queenie, I'm soooooooooo tired I can hardly move.' (He called her 'Queenie' because she was the High Queen of the whole of Ireland.)

'Ye poor soul!' said Queenie. 'You have a wee lie in while I go downstairs and make you a big Ulster fry for yer breakfast.'

She climbed out of bed, put on her green wellington boots, went down to the kitchen, poked the fire and started to cook. She put a frying pan on a crook and crane over the fire and added a dollop of fat, twelve slices of bacon, ten pieces of soda bread, six eggs and twenty pieces of potato bread. (King Brian Boru had a good appetite, so he had!) When she'd finished she guldered (shouted), 'BRIAN COME DOWN FOR YER BREAKFAST.'

King Brian was so excited at the thought of a big fry he let out such a big loud smelly one he nearly blew his bedclothes away!

His bedclothes weren't like ours. In those days they had wolf skins instead of duvets or blankets. Ireland was once coming down with wolves and they were a nuisance. They gobbled up sheep and children, so it was a very good idea to make them into lovely soft cuddly rugs.

King Brian Boru was surprised to hear something talking. The voice sounded as if it was near the floor, so he looked down and his right toe said, 'It's a fine feisty morning, Brian!'

Brian thought, 'I'm going crazy! Toes can't talk!'

He felt frightened, so got back into bed and pulled the wolf skins over his head. After a few minutes he thought, 'I'm the High King of Ireland. I shouldn't be frightened of anything, never mind my own big feet.'

He sat up in bed and fixed his golden crown straight. He was very proud of his crown and always wore it in bed. He threw back the bedclothes and scowled at his feet.

The left toe said, 'We're fed up having to live on your stinking feet. We want to go home.'

King Brian Boru said, 'My feet aren't stinking. I'm a very clean king. I have a bath once a year.'

The right toe said, 'Bath or no bath your feet stink. We can't bear the stench and we want to go home.'

'You can't,' said King Brian Boru, 'I need you. Anyway you're stuck on my feet.'

'Ye know nothing,' replied the right toe, 'Ye've five toes on your right foot and five toes on your left foot. Five and five's ten. That's too many toes. You wouldn't miss us if you let us go home. Pull us hard and we'll come off.'

'Go on,' said the left toe, 'Give it a go. Let us go home.'

King Brian Boru began to think and think and think, although he was better at fighting than thinking.

He thought, 'If I get up and go for a piddle in the middle of the night what do I crig against the furniture? My big toe!

'When I dance a jig with Queenie and she leaps up and down in her green wellies what does she land on? My big toe!

'Maybe I'd be better off without my big toes?'

The toes shouted, 'Go on Brian! Pull us off! Pull us off!'

He didn't think anymore, he just grabbed one big toe in each hand and pulled them off. They immediately grew two little legs and a pair of arms, jumped onto the floor and shouted, 'Thank you, Brian. Ye're dead on!' and dashed out of the bedroom.

Queenie let another big yell out of her. She was not polite although she was a queen!

'BRIAN! YER EGGS ARE GETTING A SKIN ON THEM. MOVE YER BUM AND GET DOWN FOR YER BREAKFAST.'

Brian guldered, 'COMING QUEENIE', threw back the bedclothes, stepped out of bed and fell flat on his nose because toes are needed for balance.

I'm King Brian Boru's wife! I'm some pup!

Queenie heard the thump and thought, 'Brian's dropped dead!' and rushed up the stairs shouting, 'Are you all right, Brian? Are you all right?'

He was sitting on the floor sobbing, 'I can't walk 'cos I've lost my toes. I won't be able to fight 'cos I've lost my toes. I won't be able to do anything 'cos I've lost my toes!'

'Nonsense,' said Queenie, who was a very sensible woman. 'You can't have done that! People don't lose toes.'

'Look!' sobbed Brian, pointing at his feet.

'Well! That was very careless of you. Where did they go?'

'I don't rightly know. They ran out the door.'

'Well, I suppose I'd better go and find them.' And with that Queenie rushed out the bedroom door, down the stairs, through the kitchen, across the courtyard, over the drawbridge and down the road.

She was a big fat woman. (In those days, fat was a status symbol. Most people were thin because they couldn't afford much food. Queenie was very rich, so she had enough money to buy lots and lots of food. As a result, she was the biggest, fattest woman in the whole of Ireland!)

Being very fat has disadvantages because when you run all your fat jiggles. It was as well buses hadn't been invented because she'd never have been able to catch one! To tell you the honest to goodness truth, she'd be running yet if the toes hadn't stopped in the middle of the road to have a fight. They couldn't remember which one was the right toe and which one was the left toe. They were knocking the melt out of each other.

'I'm the right toe!' yelled the left toe, thumping the right toe on the nose.

'No ye're not! I'm the right toe!' yelled the right toe as it bashed the left toe in a very sensitive place.

'I'm the right toe.'

'No ye're not!'

The fight went on and on.

Queenie stood in the middle of the road and thought, 'If I try to pick the toes up they'll run away. They could run into that oat field and I wouldn't be able to see them, never mind catch them. I'll have to be crafty…'

She looked down at the toes and asked, 'What gives with you guys? Why are ye fighting?'

'We can't remember who's the right toe and who's the left toe,' they shouted.

'Why don't ye go and ask Brian? He's sure to know.'

'Good thinking!' shouted the toes, as they turned round and ran back up the road, over the drawbridge, across the courtyard, through the kitchen, up the stairs and into Brian's bedroom.

'Brian! Brian!' they yelled. 'Which one's the right toe? Which one's the right toe?'

'Come here toes, till I have a good look at you. I can't tell unless I can see you clearly. My eyesight isn't as good as it once was.'

The toes ran over to Brian, who bent down and picked them up.

'There,' he said, sticking the right toe back on his foot. 'You're the right toe. And you're the left toe,' as he stuck it back in position.

'Thanks Brian,' yelled the toes. 'Now pull us off again so we can go home.'

'I can't do that,' said Brian, 'I'm sorry toes, but I need you. I can't walk without you. You'll just have to live in my smelly socks, but I'll tell you what I'll do. I'll have a bath twice a year from now on.'

From that day until the day he was killed after the Battle of Clontarf in 1014, King Brian Boru slept with his socks on, otherwise his toes talked to each other and kept him awake at night.

If you sleep with your socks on you're descended from King Brian Boru, the High King of the whole of Ireland! He was one of the greatest kings the world has ever known and you should feel very proud.

King Brian Boru was killed after he'd fought the Vikings in the Battle of Clontarf in the year 1014. He won the battle and he was tired. So were his son and grandson, so they decided to go back to their tent and have a wee snooze.

A stupid Viking got lost, ran in the wrong direction and accidentally ended up in King Brian Boru's tent. When he saw the king snoring along with his son and grandson he cut their heads off!

King Brian Boru's friends put his body into a coffin, carried it to Armagh and buried it in the grounds of what is now St Patrick's Anglican Cathedral. If you go there you'll find a plaque on the wall of the cathedral that tells you where it lies, and if you listen very carefully you might hear the ghosts of his toes talking to each other.

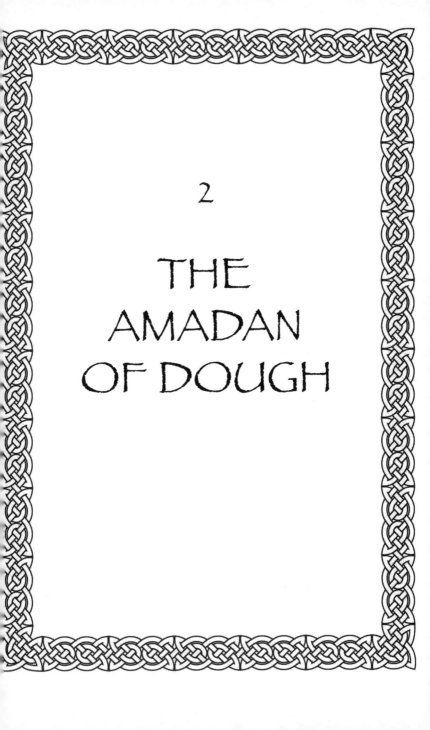

2

THE AMADAN OF DOUGH

I think the Amadan of Dough lived in Doe Castle because 'Doe' sounds like 'Dough' and spelling can change over time.

Doe Castle's on the site of a very ancient castle on the shore near a village called Creeslough in County Donegal.

The Amadan could only be described as a big edjiot. He was reckoned to be not wise, off his trolley, not right in the head, or any other way you'd describe somebody who is stupid and clumsy.

'Amadan' is Irish for stupid. He was called the Amadan of Dough because when he was a child he was growing so big he was given nothing but dough to eat in the hope that it would stunt his growth. It didn't!

When he was a teenager he was so big and clumsy he kept standing on, or tripping over, his wee brothers and sisters. His father, the king, became worried in case the Amadan killed them so he said, 'Amadan, you're a big boy now. It's time you left home.'

The Amadan said very firmly, 'I won't leave home unless you give me a sword that'll cut through a bale of straw in one slash.'

His father gave him a fantastic sword. The Amadan was as pleased as Punch with his brand new sword and swaggered off down the road with it flashing in the sunlight.

The Amadan walked for seven days and seven nights until he came to a great castle. He knocked on the door. Nobody answered so he went inside and saw a huge table laden with all sorts of delicious food. Jelly and custard, fancy cakes and puddings as well as huge slices of roast beef, chicken, ham, pheasant, turkey, stuffing, red sauce, brown sauce, cranberry sauce, vegetables, potatoes; in fact everything you could think of! The Amadan's face split into a smile that stretched from ear to ear as he sat down and ate a hearty feast.

He'd just finished eating when in came three princes. They were exhausted, bleeding from lots of wounds and their clothes had been cut to ribbons. They said, 'Every day we have to go and fight three giants! We kill them and we don't know what happens during the night! Next day there they are, as good as new, and we have to go and fight them again! It's terrible!'

'Don't worry,' said the Amadan. 'I'll go and see what's going on.'

He found the giants, Slat Mor, Slat Marr and Slat Beag, lying dead. He hid behind some rocks to see what happened.

In the middle of the night, the old Cailleach of the Rocks appeared. (A Cailleach's a very ugly, very old woman, a sort of a witch.) She had four badachs (that means big, ignorant fellows) with her and she carried a huge feather and a jar of iocshlainte ointment (that's a magic healing ointment). She used the feather to put a little ointment on each of the giants, Slat Mor, Slat Marr and Slat Beag. They immediately sprang back to life.

The Amadan rushed out from behind the rock, raised his sword and began to fight.

It was a tough fight. It made the hard ground soft, the soft ground spring into wells, the rocks turn into pebbles and the pebbles turn into gravel that fell all over the countryside like hailstones. All the birds of the air and the animals of the north and south came to watch.

At the end of the fight Slat Mor, Slat Marr, Slat Beag, the four badachs and the old Cailleach of the Rocks lay dead.

The Cailleach of the Rocks said, with her dying breath, 'I put you under a geasa (That's a very serious thing. It means you must do what you're told or be cursed for all time.) to go and fight the Black Bull of the Brown Wood.'

The Amadan put some of the iocshlainte ointment on his wounds and was immediately as right as rain. He set off down the road to find the Black Bull of the Brown Woods.

He walked and walked and walked until he came to a peculiar hut at the edge of the forest. It didn't have a roof, just a big feather hanging over it. A Rough Red Woman was standing in the doorway. She said, 'You're the Amadan of Dough, the King of Ireland's son, aren't you? How's about you? What have you done and where are you going?'

The Amadan said, 'I had a great fight. I fought and killed the three giants Slat Mor, Slat Marr and Slat Beag, the four badachs and the old Cailleach of the Rocks, who, with her dying breath, put me under a geasa to kill the Black Bull of the Brown Wood.'

'Oh dear! Oh dear! Oh dear!' said the Rough Red Woman, 'Yon's desperate! Nobody's managed to fight the Black Bull of the Brown Wood and live to tell the tale. Never mind. Come on, on in and have a wee bite to eat and a bed for the night.'

The Amanda was very polite, apart from the fact that he farted like a motorbike and belched like a volcano, so he said, 'That's very nice of you. Thank you very much indeed.'

The Rough Red Women gave him a big feed and a comfortable bed. Next day, when he'd had a hearty breakfast, she said, 'My poor Amadan, no one's ever fought the Black Bull of the Brown Wood and come back alive! I'll tell you what to do. When you reach the Brown Woods the Black Bull will charge down the hill like a hurricane. Take this cloak

Give me a feather instead of a roof any day.

and throw it over a large rock. Hide behind it. The Black Bull will charge the rock, hit his head and stun himself. Jump on its back and fight for your life. If you survive, come and see me. If you're dead, I'll come and find you.'

The Amadan thanked her and took the cloak. He walked and walked and walked until he came to the Brown Wood. The Black Bull came charging down the hill. The Amadan put the cloak over a large rock. The Black Bull hit his head with a mighty clang and roared with fury. The Amadan leapt upon the animal's back and slashed away with his sword.

It was a tough fight. It was so tough they made the hard ground soft, the soft ground spring into wells, the rocks turn into pebbles and the pebbles turn into gravel that fell all over the countryside and came down like hailstones. All the birds of the air and the animals of the north and south came to watch. Eventually, the Amadan managed to stick his sword through the Black Bull's heart. With its dying breath the Black Bull said, 'I put you under a geasa to fight the Beggar Man of the King of Sweden.'

The Rough Red Woman was very pleased when she saw the Amadan running down the road towards her. She smiled as he boasted, 'I have killed the three giants, Slat Mor, Slat Marr and Slat Beag, the old Cailleach of the Rocks and her four badachs and the Black Bull of the Brown Wood, who put me under a geasa to fight the Beggar Man of the King of Sweden.

'Oh dear! Oh dear! Oh dear!' said the Rough Red Woman, 'Yon's desperate! My poor Amadan! Nobody's ever managed to fight the Beggar Man of the King of Sweden and live to tell the tale. Never mind. Come on, on in and I'll give you a wee bite to eat and a comfortable bed for the night and tell you what to do.'

Next day, when he'd had a hearty breakfast, the Rough Red Woman said, 'The Beggar Man of the King of Sweden will come down from the sky in a cloud. You'll be able to see the whole world between his legs and nothing above his head. If he thinks he's losing the fight, he'll go up into the sky in a mist and refresh himself. You may let him go up once, but if you let him go a second time he'll kill you when he comes back down again.

'My poor Amadan, I fear you'll not come back alive. If you survive, come back and see me. If you're dead, I'll come and find you.'

The Amadan thanked her and went on his way. He walked and walked and walked until he saw a great cloud. The Beggar Man of the King of Sweden was hanging from it. The Amadan saw the whole world between his legs and nothing above his head. The Beggar Man of the King of Sweden drew his sword, screamed, 'Wait 'til I get you!' and rushed at the Amadan.

It was a tough fight. It made the hard ground soft, the soft ground spring into wells, the rocks turn into pebbles and the pebbles turn into gravel that fell all over the countryside like hailstones. All the birds of the air and the animals from the north and south came to watch.

The fight was so fierce it made the Beggar Man of the King of Sweden feel weak, so he whistled and disappeared up into the clouds to refresh himself. When he came down he fought even harder than before. After a while he became tired and whistled for the cloud to take him up into the sky for a second time.

The Amadan remembered what the Rough Red Woman had told him, so he leapt into the air and drove his sword through the Beggar Man of the King of Sweden's heart. With his dying breath the Beggar Man of the King of Sweden said, 'I put you under a geasa to fight the Silver Cat of the Seven Glens.'

The Amadan used the feather to anoint his wounds with iocshlainte ointment and instantly became as right as rain, so he returned to the Rough Red Woman who asked, 'What have you done?'

'I have killed the three giants, Slat Mor, Slat Marr and Slat Beag, the old Cailleach of the Rocks and her four badachs, the Brown Bull of the Black Woods and the Beggar Man of the King of Sweden, who put me under a geasa to kill the Silver Cat of the Seven Glens.'

The Rough Red Woman burst into tears. 'Oh dear! Oh dear! Oh dear! Yon's desperate! My poor Amadan! Nobody's ever fought the Silver Cat of the Seven Glens and lived to tell the tale.

'Never mind. Come on, on, on in and I'll give you a wee bite to eat and a comfortable bed for the night.'

After a hearty breakfast the Rough Red Woman told the Amadan how to find the Silver Cat of the Seven Glens and said, 'There is only one place where that cat can be killed. It's a black spot on the bottom of its stomach.

'My poor Amadan. I fear you'll not come back alive. If you survive, come and see me. If you're dead, I'll come and find you. I'll cover my well in a layer of honey and watch how the fight's going. If the well turns red I'll know the cat's winning. If it's covered in honey I'll know you're winning.'

The Amadan of Dough set out to find the Silver Cat of the Seven Glens and found her cave. She came out at 12 o'clock and let a roar out of her that drove back the waters of the sea and piled them a mile high. She spat at the Amadan and snarled, 'Who are you?'

'I'm the Amadan of Dough. I fought and killed the three giants, Slat Mor, Slat Marr and Slat Beat. I killed the old Cailleach of the Rocks and her four badachs, the Black Bull of the Brown Woods and the Beggar Man of the King of Sweden, who put me under a geasa to kill the Silver Cat of the Seven Glens.'

'And here you die!' growled the Silver Cat of the Seven Glens as she leapt towards the Amadan.

The other fights had been tough, but this was the worst fight ever. They fought until the hard ground turned soft, the soft ground sprang into wells, the rocks turned into pebbles and the pebbles turned into gravel that fell all over the countryside like hailstones. All the birds of the air and the animals of the north and south came to watch.

The Rough Red Woman was worried about the Amadan of Dough, so she spent the whole day watching her well. Sometimes it was covered in honey and sometimes it was the colour of blood. She cheered when the Amadan was winning and cried whenever he was losing. As night fell the well was red on one side and honey-coloured on the other. The Rough Red Woman

Yon's desperate! The well is covered in blood!

sobbed, 'Oh dear! Oh dear! Of dear! My poor Amadan! I think you've been killed!' And so he had.

The Amadan and the Silver Cat of the Seven Glens were exhausted after they'd been fighting for more than twelve hours. The Amadan lost his footing and slipped. The Silver Cat of the Seven Glens saw its opportunity and hit the top of the Amadan's head with the spike on the end of her tail and dragged it down through his body. She split the poor Amadan from head to toe. The Silver Cat of the Seven Glens opened her mouth wide and gave a loud cry of triumph. As he was dying the Amadan of Dough looked up and saw the black spot on the bottom of her stomach. He remembered what the Rough Red Woman had said. As his body fell apart he made a tremendous effort and thrust his sword down the Silver Cat of the Seven Glen's throat. The animal dropped dead and fell beside the Amadan.

The Rough Red Woman found the Amadan lying on his back with the Silver Cat of the Seven Glens in a heap beside him. She pushed the cat to one side and her hair stood on end when she saw the Amadan was split into two bloody halves. Then she spotted the bottle of iocshlainte ointment sticking out of his pocket. She hoked (poked) it out and used the feather to paint his wounds. The Amadan immediately became as right as rain. He leapt to his feet and shouted, 'I'm the Amadan of Dough. I killed the four giants Slat Mor, Slat Marr and Slat Beag, the old Cailleach of the Rocks and her four badachs, the Black Bull of the Brown Woods, the Beggar Man of the King of Sweden and the Silver Cat of the Seven Glens.'

The Rough Red Woman smiled and said, 'Amadan, you'll be the quare pup when you grow a tail!'

The Amadan looked at the Rough Red Woman and farted. She said, 'Amadan, you're stinkin!'

He said, 'I know and I love it!' and she said, 'I love it too!'

The Amadan of Dough looked at the Rough Red Woman and she didn't look either so rough or so red to him. In fact, she looked

Will ye look at the way yon big edjiot keeps kissing yon
Rough Red Woman!

beautiful! He did a big loud smelly one, gave her a kiss and said, 'Come on and we'll go and tell the three princes what I've done.'

When they saw the three princes, the Amadan said, 'I am the Amadan of Dough. I fought and killed the three giants Slat Mor, Slat Marr and Slat Beag, the old Cailleach of the Rocks and her three badachs, the Black Bull of the Brown Woods, the Beggar Man of the King of Sweden and the Silver Cat of the Seven Glens.'

The three princes were so pleased they gave the Amadan and his Rough Red Woman half their kingdom and they all lived happily ever after.

It just goes to show that no matter how stupid you are (and the Amadan was very stupid), if you try hard enough you can get everything you could possibly want.

3

BRICU'S
PARTY

ricu's a peculiar name isn't it? That's because he was a Celt and Celts had peculiar names.

Your teachers may have told you about Celts, but I bet you weren't told they didn't wear knickers (they hadn't been invented. Queen Victoria popularised wearing knickers!) and they took all their clothes off and painted their bodies blue with a dye called woad before going to war! Think how scary that was! Being attacked by a bunch of naked men, brandishing swords and shields with all their wobbly bits bouncing up and down!

My wee granny used to tell me stories about the Celts and she told me about Bricu's party.

She said Bricu was a nasty man, full of wee and wind! When he was cross he caused trouble, and he was nearly always cross.

One day he went to his wife and said, 'I'm the most reasonable of men, wealthy, good looking, an excellent warrior, yet King Conor and the Men of Ulster don't like me.

I don't know why they're mean to me but I'll get my own back. I'll build a castle on my land at Dundrum. It'll be the greatest castle in Ireland. It'll be a wheeker! I'll invite King Conor and the Men of Ulster to a party and cause them, and their po-faced wives, to fight to the death.

'I'll bet,' he muttered, 'the Men of Ulster won't want to sit with me. They don't trust me! The pigs! They'll eat my food, drink my booze and not talk to me. I'll build myself a sunroom with a window overlooking the hall. That way I'll be able to watch the swine sup their swill.'

He built his castle, made a throne for King Conor set with precious stones and put twelve seats for the twelve heroes of Ulster round it. He covered the walls with bronze overlaid with gold. He bought rich beds, pillows, quilts and coverings and arranged for a good supply of food and drink. Then he went to see King Conor and the Men of Ulster.

Conor scowled when he saw Bricu, then did his best to smile and said, 'Good to see you Bricu! How can I help you?'

Bricu gritted his teeth. 'The hypocrite!' he thought. 'An angel to my face and a devil behind my back.'

He bowed low and said, 'Greetings, oh king! I want to invite you and the Men of Ulster to a party in my new dun.' (A dun doesn't sound very exciting, does it? It was what we would think of as a palace today.)

King Conor smelt trouble but knew a refusal would be dangerous, so he said, 'I'd be delighted to accept your kind invitation, if my warriors'll come, too.'

He was crafty. He knew the Men of Ulster didn't like Bricu. He was right. When he told them about Bricu's invitation they shouted, 'We're not going near Bricu! He's a parcel of bad meat. He'll make us fight.'

Bricu let out a loud smelly one when King Conor told him what the Men of Ulster had said and snarled, 'How could I make the Men of Ulster fight? I just want to show them my cool new home.

'If they're scared of me I'll sit in my sunroom and watch through the window. If they don't come, I'll cause trouble. I'll make father fight son, mother fight daughter! I'll make the women so annoyed their boobs'll bang together in rage!'

So the Men of Ulster accepted Bricu's invitation. Bricu was delighted.

He went to see a warrior called Laegaire and said, 'You should be Champion of Ulster and be given the champion's portion at my party. It's worth having – a huge vat of wine, a whole boar and a whole fatted calf!'

Laegaire said, 'I'll fight for it!'

Bricu loved to hear warriors saying they'd fight. He went to talk to Conall and said, 'It's great to see you. You deserve the Champion's portion at my party. It's a huge vat of wine and the finest meat in Ireland.' Conall said, 'I'll fight for it if necessary.'

Then Bricu went to talk to Cuculan. 'Look at you!' he said, 'Look at those muscles!

No man in Ulster can match them. The champion's portion at my party should be yours. You're better than the others.'

Cuculan said, 'That's true, I'll knock the melt out of anyone who tries to keep it from me!'

Bricu was delighted and did a lot of wee smelly ones to celebrate.

Bricu welcomed the Men of Ulster when they arrived at his castle in Dundrum, near Newcastle, on the road going round the coast towards Downpatrick, in County Down. He spread out the feast, then said, 'I'll let you decide who gets the champion's portion,' and left the room.

Laegaire's chariot driver jumped to his feet.

'Give it to Laegaire,' he shouted, 'no one deserves it better.'

'It should go to Conall!' yelled Conall's chariot driver.

Laeg, Cuculan's chariot driver, bawled, 'Cuculan's the best warrior. It should go to him.'

Laegaire, Conall and Cuculan began to fight.

King Conor was horrified. It wasn't fair. Laegaire and Conall were attacking Cuculan.

After a few minutes Sencha, the Druid (a Druid's a kind of wizard) said, 'I think we could separate those fellows now. They've had time to defend their honour and they'll probably be glad of an excuse to stop fighting and get stuck into eating and drinking.'

'You're right!' exclaimed King Conor. He got between the men and shouted, 'That's enough lads! We're supposed to be enjoying ourselves, not knocking the melt out of each other. Why don't you share the champion's portion?'

The men agreed, sat down near the fire, ate, drank and made merry.

Bricu groaned, 'Oh no! Look! King Conor and Sencha have stopped those fools fighting. May the hens of hell roost on their chests!' He was very disappointed. 'Hells, bells and buckets of blood!' he snarled, 'I've wasted my money having a party. I wanted those hooligans to kill each other.'

He sat muttering to himself, wondering how he could make trouble.

'What can I do, I wonder? ... I've got it! Those stupid louts are proud of their

I'll get yon women fighting!

pasty wives … if I set the women fighting, they'll follow!'

He sidled outside and saw Fidelma, Laegaire's wife, coming out for a breath of fresh air. He swarmed up to her and said, 'Fidelma, you're absolutely gorgeous! No wonder Laegaire's so proud of you. You should be recognised as the first woman in the land. Now let me give you a bit of advice. Make sure that no woman walks through the door in front of you. Claim your rightful position. It reflects on your husband, doesn't it? Don't let him down.'

'Thank you Bricu,' blushed Fidelma. 'You're right! My husband's a great warrior. I should look worthy of him.'

Bricu was pleased. He smirked as he sat down in the sunroom.

Lendabar, Conall's wife, came outside and walked towards him. Bricu smiled like a cat with cream.

'How are you, my beauty?' he asked, 'You're gorgeous. You should be the first woman in the land.'

She, like Fidelma, agreed and went on her way.

Bricu was delighted.

Cuculan's wife, Emer, appeared.

Bricu kissed her cheek and said she would help Cuculan's claim to become Champion of Ulster by acting as the first lady in the land.

Emer thanked him.

Bricu was very happy. There was bound to be a fight, so he did a big loud smelly one!

The three women met and chatted before deciding to go back to the party. They began walking slowly, each watching the others closely to make sure she'd be the first to enter the building. As they got nearer they walked faster. They ended up running with their skirts hitched up past their knees, their necks stretched out and their cloaks flying behind so you could see their bare bottoms.

Bricu stood in the window of his sun-room and laughed, 'Stupid women! They look like geese in flight. Ha! Ha! Ha!'

The noise of the women running sounded like chariots. Sencha saw them and shouted, 'Bricu has made the women fight. Shut the doors! They'll kill us!'

The heavy doors slammed shut.

Emer arrived first and demanded to be let in to honour her husband.

Then Fidelma yelled, 'My husband's a mighty warrior! I should come in first so he's recognised as Champion.'

Lendabar guldered, 'My husband's the greatest! I should be first.'

Emer yelled, 'No you shouldn't. Cuculan, my husband, is the Hound of Ulster, so I should be the first to enter.'

Cuculan flew into a rage when he heard Emer's voice. He lifted the house wall up in the air so Emer was able to walk in through the gap. He was so pleased to see her, he dropped the wall. It sank into the earth, causing Bricu's sun-room to collapse. He and his wife fell out into a big pile of dog's poo.

Bricu was furious. He picked himself up and guldered, 'What do you think you're up to? I invited you to my party and you've wrecked my home. I put you under a geasa.' (You remember what that is, don't you? It's a very serious promise. Something you must do, or be cursed for ever) 'You mustn't leave here until you fix it!'

The Men of Ulster tried to straighten the walls. They couldn't, so they said to Cuculan, 'You broke it. You fix it. And hurry up! We're starving.'

Cuculan took a deep breath, a firm grip of the wall and heaved. Gradually the wall rose up until it stood as straight as before. Everyone cheered before sitting down and enjoying Bricu's feast. As for Bricu – he went and washed the dog's poo off himself and his wife.

(Loughbrickland's on Northern Ireland's A1 dual carriageway, about 2 miles from Banbridge. You'll see a lake with a funny looking island, called a crannog, in the middle. Bricu lived on the crannog in 'once upon a time' sort of time before he built his castle in Dundrum. Loughbrickland village is on the other side of the dual carriageway. It's called after Bricu.

Dundrum's on the South Down coast. Bricu's palace would have been built of wood and woven branches. Over time it was replaced by a stone castle and its ruins are on the site. You can climb around them.)

4

A FEARFUL
FRIGHT AT
THE PROLEEK
DOLMEN

Dolmens look peculiar. They're huge structures that, from a distance, look like monsters. They're made of two gigantic boulders with a huge flat boulder on top, so if you use your imagination they look like a door. The Celts thought of them as a door to the Otherworld, which was their idea of heaven.

If you want to see the Proleek Dolmen, go to a roundabout on the main road between Dundalk and Newry and look for a signpost pointing to Ballymascanlon and Carlingford. Turn down that road until you come to a sign, on the left of the road, that says, 'Ballymascanlon Hotel'. Go along that narrow tree-lined driveway and into the car park. You'll see a sign pointing to the Proleek Dolmen.

Years ago, people had crazy ideas. They didn't believe that after you die your spirit goes to heaven. They thought you went to the Otherworld. They also thought there are special places in the world where it's possible to go into the Otherworld and that it was possible to go there and come back again!

Dolmens are graves of very important people. They're built like huge doors, so the souls of those very important people could pass through it after death. They are very old. The Proleek Dolmen's older than the Egyptian pyramids. Isn't that something?

Folklore says you shouldn't visit old places at night in case ghosts or the fairies get you! I don't believe that but I'm not going anywhere near an old place at night just in case!

I like visiting the Proleek Dolmen because it looks weird, like a prehistoric monster with loose stones sitting on top of it. The oral tradition says if you make a wish and throw a stone up and it stays on the capstone then your wish'll come true.

I like throwing stones and there aren't many places you can throw them without getting into trouble! I must have thrown hundreds of stones at the capstone. (I was always very careful not to hit anyone!)

One day I took my friends, Jack and Tom, to the Proleek Dolmen. We each lifted a stone and threw it up on top of the capstone.

Will my wish come true?

My stone fell down immediately, as did Tom's, but Jack's stayed in place.

Tom laughed and said, 'Doreen, the dolmen doesn't like us. We've no chance of our wishes coming true!'

Jack went white and said, 'That thing's evil! It grabbed my stone. I've got to get out of here!' and he started to run back down the path.

Tom and I laughed. We thought he was a right edjiot being frightened by three big boulders!

The next time I went to the Proleek Dolmen I made a wish and threw a stone up. I felt as if the dolmen grabbed it and pulled my hand. It was a very strange feeling. It gave me a fearful fright! It scared me so much I nearly wet my knickers! And I'll tell you something – I'm never going to throw a stone at that capstone again.

5

DUNLUCE CASTLE'S KITCHEN FALLS INTO THE SEA

L ady MacDonnell was upset when her husband insisted they move into Dunluce Castle. She said, 'I don't like the haunted atmosphere and I don't like the way it's perched on the edge of a cliff. It's dangerous. It could fall into the sea.'

Her husband said, 'You've got too much imagination, my dear. The castle's a beautiful place and the view's stunning! It's been the headquarters of the Clan MacDonnell since the sixteenth century. Now I'm the head of the clan we have to live there. We've no choice.'

Lady MacDonnell made the best of a bad job. She did everything expected of her. She organised an efficient household and entertained many guests. But she was right. The castle was haunted. She often heard somebody crying in the castle's north-eastern turret and when she opened the door there was nobody there.

Sometimes she saw a white figure running down the stairs and she was often aware of a presence. She said nothing because she knew her husband would tell her to wise up because her imagination was playing tricks on her. But it wasn't. The castle was haunted by the ghost of Maeve Roe MacQuillan, who was the only daughter of Lord MacQuillan.

In those days fathers could marry daughters off to anyone they liked. It didn't matter what the daughter thought, she had to either like it or lump it!

Maeve Roe wanted to marry Reginald O'Cahan and her father said she had to marry Richard Oge.

Maeve Roe hated Richard. He was very old and very ugly, with rotten teeth and bad manners. He did a lot of big loud smelly ones, belched frequently and his breath was stinking. He was not fit. Maeve refused to have anything to do with him!

Her father was livid with rage. 'You'll do as I say,' he yelled, 'or spend the rest of your life locked up in one of the turrets!'

Maeve Roe was like me. She was very stubborn. She wouldn't agree to marry Richard Oge, so her father imprisoned her in a small turret room.

When she was locked up, Maeve Roe asked for some white wool and began knitting a dress. She was asked if she was knitting her wedding dress and snarled, 'It's not my wedding dress. It's my shroud.'

'Roe' means 'red'. Maeve Roe had red hair and a fiery temper and she was very stubborn. She was not going to marry Richard Oge! No way! She would die locked up in the tower if need be. She spent her time knitting and gazing out of the window, hoping against hope that Reginald O'Cahan could come and rescue her. Days turned into weeks and weeks turned into months, and poor Maeve Roe remained locked in her tiny round room.

Maeve Roe's father became worried. She was his only daughter. He loved her and was sorry he'd locked her up. But he had his pride and felt he couldn't tell anyone he was sorry, so he hatched a cunning plan. He asked his pageboy to pretend to steal the key of the door to Maeve's room, give it to Richard O'Cahan, arrange for a rowing boat to be beside the mermaid's cave, which is underneath the castle, and help the young couple escape.

The pageboy did as he was asked. Unfortunately a huge storm blew up, the young couple's boat capsized and they were drowned.

Richard O'Cahan's body washed up on the shore several days later but Maeve's body was never found. Her ghost haunts the castle and it behaves like a banshee. Banshees watch their families and howl if they think the family's in danger. A banshee's cry usually, but not always, says somebody's going to die. People have been known to wet themselves, and worse, when they hear a banshee crying! It's a scary sound.

It was a windy night. The Lady MacDonnell in this story was expecting visitors when she heard Maeve Roe cry and thought, 'Something terrible's going to happen. That terrible noise is the banshee. There's no point in telling my husband. He'd just tell me to "catch myself on" and "stop being stupid". I can't do anything, so I'd better go ahead and organise the banquet.'

The storm turned into a tempest. Rain lashed down, the sea roared as it hit the rocks below the castle, the wind howled and raged.

Lady MacDonnell became more and more worried. She caught a glimpse of a white figure running up the corridor. She was so frightened that if she hadn't been a lady she'd have wet her knickers, but she was a lady so she didn't!

(Do you remember I told you in the story about Bricu's party that nobody wore knickers until Queen Victoria made them popular? This story happened in the 1850s. Lady MacDonnell was very posh so she was like the queen and wore knickers.)

'I still won't marry Richard Oge! Won't! Won't! Won't!'

All the guests arrived safely and Lady MacDonnell breathed a sigh of relief. They had a glass of sherry and sat down to dinner. They appeared to be enjoying themselves, when there was an ear-shattering sound followed by loud crashing noises. A great wind hurled round the banqueting room and blew all the candles out. (This was before electricity had been invented.) It became cold and dark. Everyone screamed. The servants came running. They were hysterical. 'The kitchen's fallen into the sea!' they screamed. 'The kitchen's fallen into the sea!'

Everybody in the kitchen was drowned, all except one little boy who was brushing a corner.

There was no dinner that night. The guests went home hungry and the MacDonnells moved to Glenarm. They still live there in Glenarm Castle. They don't go raiding castles or fighting wars any more. They've settled down and Hector McDonnell is a world-famous artist. There's a beautiful garden around their castle in Glenarm. It's open to

We had no dinner that night!

the public and you can get a nice cup of tea in the tea-room.

Dunluce Castle is a ruin that is also open to the public. You can walk inside its derelict walls, visit Maeve Roe's room and see its round walls and small window. It feels haunted. Visitors to the castle sometimes see her ghost sitting in the window and she may come out of her room at night and brush the floor.

Maeve Roe is a banshee for the Mac-Donnells as well as the MacQuillans because one of her ancestors married a MacDonnell. The MacDonnells captured the castle in the 1500s when Sorley Boy MacDonnell brought his mates over from Islay. They climbed up the steep cliffs around the castle and threw the MacQuillans out!

6

THE TAILOR
AND THE
WITCH

I find it very sad to know that, in the past, if you couldn't work you could starve to death. There was no national assistance of any kind, no job seekers, or disability allowance, no pension. There was little, if any, help apart from what your family and friends could give you. The trouble was they might not have anything to spare because they probably were poor and starving, too.

Most people worked on the land. You need to be strong and healthy to be able to do that. If you were disabled then some sort of job you could do was found for you. Blind people often became musicians, while girls with bad legs or sore backs often became seamstresses.

Seamstresses travelled around the country and stayed in people's homes. Their job was to make new curtains and to turn dresses. That means they picked old shabby dresses apart and sewed them up again with the inside outside so they looked like new. Another thing they might be asked to do was turn old coats and dresses into patchwork quilts or rag rugs. Nothing was ever wasted.

Disabled boys often trained as tailors. They travelled around the country and stayed with people in the same way as the seamstresses, except they usually tailored new suits and dresses from new cloth.

There once was a tailor who had a bad leg and every two years he went to stay with a strange woman in County Tyrone near the border with Fermanagh. She lived in a one-room cottage with a half-loft and slept in a settle bed near the fire. (A settle bed is a big box with a back on it. It looks like a wooden settee during the day. At night it's opened out to form a bed. A straw mattress and bedclothes are stored inside it.)

The woman used the half-loft for storage. She made a spare bed up there with a bag of straw for a mattress and a blanket. The tailor struggled up a ladder and slept there at night. When he was lying in the loft he could peep over the edge and see the room below.

One spring morning he woke up early and heard a strange noise. A sort of MMMMMMM, mmmmmmmm,

MMMMMMMMMM, mmmmmmm. He peeped over the edge of the loft and saw the woman jump into a big pot of water. A hare leapt out the other side and ran out the door. The tailor thought, 'I'm dreaming,' and went back asleep. When he woke up again the old woman was making porridge and the large pot was tucked away at the side of the fire. Everything appeared normal.

The tailor worked all day. As he sewed, he watched her out of the side of his eye. The more he watched, the stranger she seemed. She had a very pointy nose and a pointy chin. He wondered if she was a witch? He wondered if he'd been dreaming or had he seen her turn into a hare? He decided to wake up early next day and watch.

Next day he woke early, moved quietly over to the edge of the half-loft and watched and waited. He saw the old woman get out of bed, go under the half-loft to get dressed, pull the large pot out of the corner, put it in front of the fire and fill it with water from the buckets sitting beside the door. (In those days water had to be carried from wells, springs, rivers or ponds. It was kept in buckets inside the house beside the door.)

The woman walked three times round the pot making the strange MMMMMMM, mmmmmmmmmm, MMMMMMMM, mmmmmmm sound. She jumped into the pot and a hare came out the other side. The tailor was so excited he let out a big loud smelly one. 'Blimey!' he thought, 'I'm glad I didn't fart when the old woman was inside the cottage. She'd have heard me!' She'd have known I was awake! I think she'd have been furious. She might have put an evil spell on me. But I was right. I am staying in a witch's house.'

He felt a bit frightened as he lay back on the bag of straw and waited. At last he heard the hare come back. He watched as it jumped into the pot and the woman appeared out the other side.

The tailor was very excited. He pretended to be asleep and was very careful not to do any loud or smelly ones. 'I wonder,' he thought, 'where the witch goes when she's turned into a hare?

'Witches are evil. They put curses on cows so their milk can't be turned into butter. That's a terrible thing to do. You need butter to put on your spuds. I wonder if the water'd turn me into a hare? I wonder if I could follow her, find out what she's up to. Maybe I could find out how to keep her from putting curses on cows?' He sat sewing and thinking all day and eventually decided to jump into the water

A wicked witch stole my butter!

next day and see what happened.

That night the tailor didn't take his trousers off when he went to bed. He wanted to be able to jump quickly out of bed in the morning.

He heard the woman pull the cooking pot in front of the fire. He watched as she jumped in and reappeared as a hare. He half slithered and half fell down the ladder, jumped into the cooking pot and came out as a hare. He rushed to the door and was just in time to see the witch disappear through a hole in the hedge. He ran after her and followed her over a field, through another hedge and up a hill. When he reached the top he saw hundreds of hares having a meeting. He joined them. A big hare in the middle of the group wiggled its nose and shouted, 'I smell danger! There's a stranger in our midst!' The hares immediately scattered and ran back home. He ran down the hill, through the hedge and into the house and was just in time to see a hare jump into the water and the woman appear out the other side, lift the pot and throw the water out.

He was lucky because the water hit and washed over him. He immediately turned into a man again.

The woman was raging. She yelled, 'How dare you! I've a good mind to turn you back into a hare.'

The tailor was so scared he nearly pooed his pants. 'Ppppppplease don't do that!' he stuttered, 'My family'd worry about me. They'd come and look for me. They know I'm working for you. I promise never to tell anyone. I won't charge for the work I've done. I'll leave immediately.'

The woman scowled at him and thought, 'It could be awkward if his family came looking for him.' She snarled, 'Collect your things and go. I've put a spell on you. If you ever say anything about what happened today you'll turn into a hare. Now get out!'

The tailor quietly collected his things and went to his next house. It was a lovely place, full of children and laughter. They gave him a comfortable seat in the kitchen and a big bowl of delicious Irish stew. Then he started to work, making a new suit for the youngest son. He was sewing away when one of the children came up to him and asked, 'What have you got behind your ear? It looks like fur.' He put his hand up to his head and screamed! He'd a patch of fur behind his ear.

Eventually the tailor fell in love and got married. He and his wife had seventeen children. Each child had a patch of animal fur behind its ear. If you've a bit of fur behind your ear you're descended from the tailor. Do you have one?

7

THE
STRANGE
CELTS

D o you remember the story I told you about Bricu's party? I said the Celts had peculiar ideas compared with the way we live today. Didn't I tell you they loved to fight and took all their clothes off and dyed their bodies blue before they went to war? They thought it was a good idea to be killed in battle because their souls would go straight to heaven, which they called the Otherworld.

They were real bizarre people who wove round houses out of branches and slept in a circle round a fire in the middle of the floor with their feet towards the fire. Its smoke went out of a hole in the middle of the roof. They had to be careful not to move down the bed during the night or they'd have burnt their toes in the fire. They also had a weird way of crowning a king. There were no churches, never mind big important ones like Westminster Abbey, so they couldn't have what we would think of as a proper coronation. They had a great feast instead, and the Celts didn't have one Irish king – they had 200!

Conor was a famous king so I'm going to tell you how he and all the other Celtic kings were crowned before Christianity arrived in Ireland.

The celebrations began early in the morning when all of Conor's subjects prepared a cooking pot. They didn't have anything like stoves or the pots and pans we cook our food in today. There was no gas or electricity or water on tap. It's difficult to cook without such things and for an important event like a coronation they had a real problem because they wanted to cook a horse! I don't mean just a bit of a horse, I mean the whole horse! (Celts usually ate pork and a feed of horse was a special treat!) Did you ever hear anyone say, 'I could eat a horse?' They did!

To cook the horse they dug a really big hole in the ground, beside a river or a bog so water seeped into it.

Cold water's no good for cooking, so it had to be heated up to boiling point. The Celts collected a lot of wood and lots of rocks and stones and lit a big fire. Collecting lots and lots of wood and attending a fire's hard work. It's easy to do hard work if it feels like fun, so the Celts did something really crafty. They hired musicians to play fast tunes to make people feel like dancing and singing. That made the whole atmosphere jolly, like a good party, as they heated the stones, making them red hot, and then used sticks to push them into the 'cooking pot' so they heated the water!

When the water was boiled, the future king took all his clothes off, put a halter on a white horse and ran, leading the horse, up to the cooking pot. The horse was slaughtered, its body parts cut up, wrapped in straw and thrown into the pot.

After the horse was cooked, cold water was added to it so the 'pot' could be used as a bath. The king, who you will remember was naked, got a drinking vessel (something like a large cow's horn), jumped into the water, filled the cow's horn with 'bath' water and drank it. Everybody laughed and cheered! The king filled the 'cup' with bath water and passed it round his subjects, so everyone was able to have a drink. Ugh!

Would you like you have a bath in water that had been used to cook? It must have been full of bits of straw, fat and little pieces of stuff from the horse. Disgusting! And I'm sure the king wasn't clean. It was difficult to wash in those far off times, so people didn't bother much. They might have had an occasional dip in a river or a lake.

I don't like the idea of drinking water that's had somebody's dirty feet and bum in it! Do you?

Once all his subjects had had a drink of 'bath' water, the king was crowned and he invited everybody to a party.

Conor was a good king although he did terrible things to Deidre of the Sorrows, but that's another story. When he became old and grey he said, 'I don't want to be painted blue and rush into battle, I'd just love to go and see my old friend Sobhairce in Dunseverick, sit beside his fire, drink a lot of mead and have a bit of craic.'

His friends loved him, so they helped him go to Dunseverick. (Today there's a ruined castle built on the site visited by King Conor. It's on the North Antrim Coast near the Giant's Causeway.)

Sobhairce was delighted to see Conor and the two old boys sat by the fire drinking mead, scratching and farting, when Conall Cearnach arrived from the Middle East.

I bet you don't believe a man from Ireland could travel as far as the Middle East 2,000 years ago!

Well, you'd be wrong. King Conor lived in Navan Fort, which is near the city of Armagh. When archaeologists excavated his old home they found a monkey's skull! Monkeys come from far off places.

Conall Cearnach was very upset. He sat down beside Conor and began to cry. Warriors don't cry! Warriors have to be tough and macho. Conor was astonished, but he was an old kindly man so he asked, 'What's wrong?'

Conall Cearnach said, 'I'm ashamed of myself sitting here blubbering like a baby. I'm just so glad to be home! I can't forget the terrible thing I saw.'

'What did you see?'

In between sobs, Conall Cearnach explained he'd wanted to see the world so he'd gone to England and joined the Roman army as a mercenary (a mercenary is somebody who joins the army of any country because he wants to earn money.)

Conall had been sent to Jerusalem and said, 'The Romans are cruel. They've invented a terrible way of killing people. They make a wooden cross and nail people to it. Think about that. They stretch a man's arms out and hammer nails into his hands. Then they cross his legs and break his bones by hammering a huge nail through his ankles. It's agony. You should hear the men scream. Being crucified's worse than being hacked to pieces in battle.'

King Conor did a big loud one and said, 'That's awful, but I'd have thought it wouldn't have upset a warrior like you.'

'You're right. I didn't like hammering nails into defenceless people, I can cope with that. I'm upset because we crucified the Son of God.'

'What do you mean "the Son of God"? The son of which god? Lugh, Angus Og, Balor of the Evil Eye, or any of the other gods?'

'No I don't mean our gods. They're no good. The Romans have their own gods, Jupiter, Mars, Neptune, Pluto and so on, and they're no good either. They're like our gods. They can't do anything. No, I mean the God of the Jews. The Jews say there is only one God and some of them say He sent His Son, Jesus, to earth.

'Jesus went around doing good. He could touch a blind man and make him see.

'My boss had a daughter who died. He told Jesus, who said, "Don't worry. I've healed your daughter. Go back home and give her a big hug."

'When my boss got home he found his daughter was up and running around. His wife said the poor wee soul had been laid out and they were going to bury her because she was dead. They checked the time. The minute my boss spoke to Jesus his daughter stopped being dead and jumped up as right as rain! She gave them a right shock, so she did!

'Some of the Jews hated Jesus, so they sent soldiers out in the middle of the night to capture Him. They didn't dare do that during the day because most of the people loved Him and would have caused a riot.

'Jesus wasn't doing anyone any harm. He was talking to His friends in a garden when the soldiers dragged Him away.

'Thank God I wasn't on duty that night. One of Jesus's friends cut my friend's ear off.

'Jesus said, "Don't fight the soldiers. They're just doing what they're told. This is something I have to suffer." He touched my friend's bleeding head and his ear was fixed like brand new.

'I'm sure we crucified the Son of God. It was dreadful. We shouldn't have killed Him. We should have listened to what He said.

'The way He suffered was awful. I'll never forget it. I'll never get over it. It'll haunt me for the rest of my life. It's the reason I left the Roman army.

'His followers said I shouldn't blame myself. He loves us all, no matter what we do. He died so that our sins could be forgiven.

'I had to stand by and watch. The only thing I could do was dip a sponge in vinegar and wormwood and hold it on a stick up to His mouth to help ease His pain.'

Conor was very upset. 'Are you sure' he asked, 'you helped murder a man called Jesus, who you think was the Son of God? Are you really sure?'

'Yes! I'm sure.'

'He was crucified? You helped crucify Jesus, the Son of God? I've never heard the like. That's awful, just awful.'

'Yes, I'm sure the Man we crucified was the Son of God. The sky turned black when He died. There was a huge earthquake. The temple veil was torn from top to bottom. Graves were flung open and dead bodies were thrown out of them. It was terrible.'

Conor was so upset he got a bad pain in his chest. 'Man put God's Son to death,' he groaned. He was so upset his heart broke, he died in Dunseverick and folklore says he's buried in the Glens of Antrim.

8

ST PATRICK MAKES A MONSTER EXPLODE

When he was 15 years of age, St Patrick was kidnapped by pirates, sold as a slave and set to work looking after sheep on Slemish Mountain, near the North Antrim coast.

I like St Patrick because he said he was a 'miserable sinner' and he had a bad temper. He wrote two letters that survived. One is called 'Confession' and the other is his 'Letter to Coroticus'.

That's quite something, isn't it? Imagine writing letters that were so precious people kept them for hundreds and hundreds of years, copied them and passed them down from generation to generation. Eventually, copies of these letters were discovered in a wee church, called Ardpatrick, near Louth village, in County Louth.

We know Ardpatrick Church was founded by St Patrick because it's called after him. If you see a place containing the name 'Patrick', such as Downpatrick, Seapatrick, Knockpatrick, Slievepatrick and so on you know it was associated in some way with the Saint himself.

In his confession St Patrick said he was a 'miserable sinner' because before he was kidnapped he'd got up to all sorts of boyish pranks and had committed what he said was 'a terrible sin'.

St Patrick hated school and hadn't bothered learning much, which made life difficult when he wanted to go to Ireland as a missionary. He said a good education would have made it easier to talk the Pope into making him a bishop. Clergymen couldn't become missionaries unless they were bishops.

St Patrick wrote his second letter when a pirate called Coroticus kidnapped some of his converts, killed the old ones and sold the young ones as slaves. St Patrick was hopping mad and wrote saying, 'I hope the riches which you have unjustly gathered will be vomited from your belly' and 'The angel of death will hand you over to be crushed by the anger of dragons' and 'May you be killed with the viper's tongue and an unquenchable fire consume you'. That's some language from a saint isn't it?

When St Patrick came to Ireland as a missionary, he landed on the shores of Strangford Lough. In those far off times Irish people did not like strangers. They murdered them and stole their belongings.

St Patrick and his followers were spotted by a shepherd boy, who thought, 'Great! Strangers! I'll tell Chief Dichu. He'll come with his huge dog and I'll enjoy watching the strangers being eaten alive. There's nothing that dog enjoys more than the taste of human flesh and I love hearing people scream.'

When Chief Dichu set his dog on St Patrick it wagged its tail, licked St Patrick's hand and lay down to have its belly tickled!

Chief Dichu was astonished, so he did a lot of wee smelly ones and asked, 'Why didn't my dog eat you?' St Patrick said, 'Because Jesus looks after me. He keeps me from being hurt because I believe in Him and He loves me. He loves you too. He loves everybody.'

Dichu was so impressed he gave St Patrick an old barn to use as a church. The Irish word for 'barn' is 'saul'. That's how the church at

Saul got its name. There's been a place of worship on the site of that old barn ever since Saint Patrick was alive nearly 2,000 years ago.

There are a lot of strange stories about St Patrick fighting the devil and so on. I think they're good tales but I don't believe them. I believe that St Patrick was a very good man who spread Christianity in Ireland. He did most of his work in the north of Ireland and if you promise not to believe it I'll tell you one of my favourite silly stories about him.

One day when St Patrick was having a wee dander around the countryside a chieftain came running towards him shouting, 'Patrick! Patrick!' (He didn't know St Patrick would become a saint. He just knew him as 'Patrick'.) 'Help! Help! Help! My people are dying. When they go to the river to get water they become sick. Can you help?'

St Patrick looked serious and said, 'I don't know if I can help, but I'll do what I can. Show me where the problem lies.'

The chieftain was scared so his face went white, he belched loudly, did his best not to cry and stuttered, 'You, you, you dooooon't want me to coocoome, with youuuuuu, do you?'

St Patrick smiled and said, 'You can come if you like, but it's not necessary. Just tell me where to go.'

The chief breathed a sigh of relief for two reasons. He thought chiefs were so important they should keep out of danger, and although he'd been scared stiff he'd managed not to wet himself! Wetting yourself is not a good thing for chiefs to do. It makes their subjects laugh at them. Imagine how you'd feel if your teacher wet him or herself! You'd laugh your leg off, wouldn't you?

St Patrick asked the chief where the trouble was, then lifted his staff with one hand, a large wooden cross in the other, and prayed, 'Please Lord Jesus keep me safe,' and set off down the path to the River Lagan.

It was stinking. A dense yellow fog hung over it. The smell was so revolting I can't describe it. Can you imagine a stench like a mixture of piddle, poo, rotten meat and vomit, then multiply that by a hundred? Revolting! It made St Patrick break out into a sweat and feel sick and faint. He held the cross up high and kept praying. 'God, help me! Help me! Dear God keep me safe. I'm going to fight the devil and I'm terrified.'

The trees and grass around the river had turned into a black slimy mess. St Patrick had to walk very carefully because it was slippery and if he'd fallen he'd have been covered in stinking slime. He reached the river's edge and looked around. 'WHERE ARE YOU?' he shouted, 'COME OUT AND FIGHT!'

A great bubble of stinking yellow-green gas burst up from the middle of the river. A terrible half-human, half-animal monster was inside. St Patrick groaned and whispered, 'Jesus, it's as I thought. An ancient Formorian king who's turned into a devil.' (The Formorians were an ancient people who lived in Ireland until it was invaded by another ancient people called the Tuatha de Danann. There was a great battle during which most of the Formorians were killed but some escaped,

turned nasty and went to live in rivers and springs. All this happened a long time ago in once-upon-a-time kind of time, so you don't need to worry about it. Rivers, streams, springs and wells are safe now.)

The monster had a human head and eight arms like an octopus. It spat a poisonous blob at St Patrick. He ducked, the blob passed over his head, fell on the ground behind him and exploded. St Patrick retched but had faith in the power of Jesus, so he drew himself up to his full height, held the cross aloft and yelled, 'IN THE NAME OF JESUS CHRIST BE GONE.'

The creature shivered and spat another poisonous blob.

St Patrick held the cross over the stinking river waters and yelled, 'JESUS HELP ME! SHOW YOUR STRENGTH IN MY WEAKNESS.'

The creature screamed in pain, turned bright red and grew bigger and bigger until it exploded.

St Patrick breathed a sigh of relief, said, 'Thank you, Lord,' turned on his heel and went back to the chief. 'I don't think you'll have any more trouble,' he said.

9

FINN MCCOOL, THE GIANT'S CAUSEWAY AND OTHER THINGS

One day Finn McCool went for a wee dander along the North Antrim coast. It was a beautiful summer day, so he took his seven league boots off and enjoyed the gentle breeze ruffling the hairs on his legs. They waved in the air like corn in a field and it felt nice, as if he was being gently tickled, but his feet were smelly so the birds in the air flew away!

Finn looked up at the cliffs above him and thought, 'That's a great place to build an organ. I could sit there and play and sing to my heart's content. The music would echo round the cliffs and surge out across the sea. It would be fantastic!'

Finn loved to sing. The trouble was he'd a voice like a fog horn. The sound was guaranteed to make people run for miles to get away.

He spent the whole morning making the organ pipes and testing the sound. He was delighted when he'd finished. He played his organ and accompanied himself singing.

All the animals in the surrounding neighbourhood disappeared into their homes and sat with either their wings or their paws over their ears, that is, except for the crows. They can't sing and thought the noise Finn McCool was making was wonderful. They sat on the top of his organ and sang along with him.

About 3 o'clock in the afternoon Finn felt tired. He lay down on the shore, went to sleep and began to snore. His snores sounded like one clap of thunder after another. They caused the earth to tremble. The noise travelled across the Irish Sea and Benandonner, the Scottish giant, heard them. At first he was amused. He loved thunderstorms. They gave him the opportunity to grab the sky's dark clouds and bang them together. When he did that they gave off flashes of light. He was disappointed when he looked up into the sky and saw the sun shining. 'That's funny,' he thought, 'No dark clouds for me to play with. I wonder what's causing the noise?' He looked around and saw Finn McCool lying fast asleep underneath his big shiny organ on the other side of the Irish Sea. His chest was moving up and down and his favourite dog, Bran, was sitting on top of it enjoying the ride.

Benandonner was annoyed. How dare Finn McCool go to sleep and disturb the peace by snoring?

'Finn!' he shouted, 'Wake up! Quit making such a racket.'

Finn continued to snore.

Benandonner grew more annoyed. 'Finn wake up! Stop snoring. Shut yer gub!' (Gub means mouth. That's rude, isn't it? You wouldn't be rude like that, would you?)

Finn continued to snore, so Benandonner shouted: 'Fe, fi, fo, fum, Finn's got a dirty bum!'

Finn continued snoring so Benandonner took a deep breath and shouted so loudly the mountains trembled. 'FE, FI, FO, FUM, FINN'S GOT A DIRTY BUM.'

That did it! Finn woke up and wiped his eyes. 'What's that?' he muttered, 'Fe, fi, fo, fum. Did I hear right? Fe, fi, fo, fum. Finn's got a dirty bum. WHAT DID YOU SAY?'

Benandonner shouted more loudly than ever, 'FE, FI, FO, FUM, FINN'S GOT A DIRTY BUM.'

'What?'

'I SAID, FE, FI, FO, FUM, FINN'S GOT A DIRTY BUM.'

Finn McCool was so annoyed he jumped up, grabbed a handful of earth and threw it with all his might at Benandonner. He was usually a good shot but he was in such a temper he didn't take careful aim, so he missed. The land fell into the sea and formed the Isle of Man, while the hole left in Ireland filled with water and became Lough Neagh, which is the largest inland lough in the whole of the British Isles.

Benandonner nearly laughed his leg off. 'MISSED,' he yelled, 'YE COULDN'T HIT A COW UP THE BUM WITH A BAKE-BOARD!'

That was very insulting because a cow has a big bum, and a bake-board was a big flat piece of wood, – something like a bread-board but much bigger. Women used

Fee, fi, fo, fum, Finn's got a dirty bum!

to put a bake-board on top of a table and use it when they were rolling out dough to make tarts or kneading dough when they were baking bread.

Finn McCool was furious. He flew into a rage and shrieked, 'I'M COMING TO KNOCK THE STUFFING OUT OF YOU!' That's why he began building the Giant's Causeway. He wanted to get across the Irish Sea to Scotland and knock the melt out of (fight) the Scottish giant, Benandonner.

10

THE BODY IN THE CHIMNEY

This is a story said to have come to Ireland from Scotland with the people who ended up being called Ulster Scots.

A long time ago there was a very old woman. She was 41 years of age and in those days that was thought to be very old. Most people died when they were babies and the average expectancy of life was twenty-nine years.

The old woman was very lonely because her husband was dead and her children had emigrated to America. One night she filled her kettle with water, hung it up on her crook and crane and swung it over the fire. She sat down on a creepy stool and said sadly,

'Oh deary me, oh dear me,
I wish I had some company.
If I had some company,
I would make it a nice cup of tea!'

There was a great big BANG and down the chimney came a pair of big feet. They passed on either side of the kettle, which swung from side to side. Some of the water spilled out of the kettle and spat on the fire, which said, 'SSSSSS.' The feet hit the floor, hit the floor, hit the floor, hit the ceiling, hit the ceiling, hit the floor hit the ceiling, hit the floor, and landed beside a creepy stool. They swivelled round and arranged themselves with their toes pointing towards the fire.

The old woman jumped and screamed, 'Oh! Oh! Oh! I don't like you! I don't like things coming down the chimney!' and she walked around the room looking at the feet in a suspicious fashion.

The feet stayed quietly beside the fire. The old woman sat down again and forgot about them. She felt lonely and said:

'Oh deary me, oh deary me,
I wish I had some company.
If I had some company,
I would make it a nice cup of tea.'

There was a great big BANG and down the chimney came a huge pair of legs. They passed on either side of the kettle, which swung from side to side. Some of the water in the kettle spilled out and spat on the fire which said, 'SSSSSS.' The legs hit the floor, hit the ceiling, hit the floor, hit the ceiling, hit the floor, hit the ceiling, hit the floor and landed on top of the two big feet where they bent over and rested on the creepy stool.

The old woman jumped and screamed, 'Oh! Oh! Oh! I don't like you! I don't like things coming down the chimney!' She walked around the room looking at the feet and legs in a suspicious fashion.

The feet and legs sat quietly beside the fire. The old woman sat down again, began to knit and forgot about the feet and legs. She felt sad and lonely and said:

'Oh deary me! Oh deary me!
I wish I had some company.
If I had some company,
I would make it a nice cup of tea.'

There was a great big BANG and down the chimney came a huge body. It hit the kettle and knocked it off the crook and some of the water spat on the fire, which said 'SSSSSSSSSSSSS!'

The old woman grabbed the kettle, put it back on the crook and watched with horror as the body hit the floor, hit the ceiling, hit the floor, hit the ceiling, hit the floor, hit the ceiling and landed on top of the legs on the creepy stool.

I don't like big smelly feet!

She screamed, 'Oh! Oh! Oh! I don't like you! I don't like things coming down the chimney, especially if they have big smelly bare feet!'

She sat down heavily on her creepy stool and stared at the body sitting at the other side of the fireplace. It folded its hands on its lap and sat quietly. It looked like an ordinary big person, except it had no head. She watched it for a long time. It didn't move. She became bored, fell asleep and began to snore, 'Szzzzzzz, szzzzzzzzz, szzzzzzzzzzz.' She slept for a long time, woke up, stretched and forgot about the body coming down the chimney. She felt lonely and sad and said:

'Oh deary me, oh deary me,
I wish I had some company,
If I had some company,
I would make it a nice cup of tea.'

There was a great big BANG and down the chimney came a head. It hit the kettle, which swung from side to side. Some water spat out on top of the fire, which said, 'SSSSSSSSSSSSSSSS!'

The head hit the floor, hit the ceiling, hit the floor, hit the ceiling, hit the floor, hit the ceiling and ended up on top of the body sitting quietly on the creepy stool beside the fire. The old woman jumped and screamed, 'Oh! Oh! Oh!' She looked at the body sitting beside the fire. The head had hair, eyes, ears a nose and no mouth.

The old woman felt angry and yelled, 'Look at you! You come down my chimney in bits. You have a body and a head. The head has no mouth. I'm lonely and you're useless. Can you talk through your hair? No! Can you talk through your eyes? No! Can you talk through your ears? No! Can you talk through your nose? No! What do you talk through? You talk through your mouth! What do you not have? A mouth! I'm lonely. I want company, somebody to talk to. You're no good!' She stamped her feet and shouted crossly:

'Oh deary me, oh deary me,
I wish I had some company,
If I had some company,
I would make it a nice cup of tea.'

There was a big BANG and down came something that looked like a set of false teeth. They hit the floor, hit the ceiling, hit the floor, hit the ceiling, hit the floor, hit the ceiling then hit the wall, whizzed past the old woman and nearly bit her bum before they ended up on the head. The old woman saw it was a mouth with a big set of shiny teeth. She looked at it in horror. Her jaw fell open. She opened her mouth to scream.

The mouth smiled and said, 'Do you know something? I'd love a nice cup of tea!'

The old woman and the body that came down the chimney had the best night's craic ever. Then it thanked her politely, walked out the door and was never seen again.

11

ROBERT THE BRUCE AND THE SPIDER

This is a horrible story. The nicest thing in it is the spider. Yes, I know you probably don't like spiders. They aren't beautiful like butterflies. Butterflies look nice, but spiders eat insects such as nasty biting flies and things that would destroy our crops. In fact, if it weren't for spiders, insects would destroy your food and we'd all die of starvation.

This story starts with a horrible man, William the Conqueror. He lived in Normandy and wanted to be King of England. He sailed across the sea, landed in England and, in 1066, shot his cousin, King Harold, in the eye.

That's a nasty way to treat your cousin, isn't it? That nasty act made William King of England and he became known as William the Conqueror. He was a wicked king. He took land from his subjects and this caused all sorts of famines so that thousands of people starved to death. He got away with blue murder until he died in France in 1087, and what happened served him right.

William the Conqueror died because he was greedy. He ate enough food for ten people and became very, very, very fat. He had a huge belly that hung out over the top of his trousers and nearly reached his knees. When he rode a horse his belly hung over the horse's saddle. He was fighting a battle in France when his horse got frightened and reared up. The front part of its saddle stuck into his guts, ruptured them and he died a horrible death about six weeks later.

Nobody liked William the Conqueror, so his naked dead body was left lying around on the floor for weeks. Imagine having a dead body lying on the floor in your house. Dead bodies become smelly, and flies lay eggs in them that turn into maggots! Ugh! Eventually one of William's knights got fed up tripping over him and decided to take his body to Caen and bury it. Now here comes the really nasty bit. William the Conqueror's body decayed and became more and more swollen, bigger and bigger. It was huge. His belly looked like an air balloon! It wouldn't fit into his grave. His subjects decided to shove it down the hole as best they could. That was a mistake because his belly was full of stinking gas and it exploded. Everybody standing around got covered in smelly guts and went home rather than stay for the rest of the burial service. (I did warn you this was a horrible story!)

The Bruce family, like many other families, came over from Normandy to England with William the Conqueror. They married local people and became known as the Anglo-Normans.

The Bruce family, and their descendants, didn't like the way William the Conqueror had behaved and they hated the other Anglo-Normans who were around at the time. As a result, Robert the Bruce decided he wanted to chase them out of Scotland. Then he thought, 'If I chase them away they'll only come back. I'd better go to war and kill the lot of them!' He lost seven battles in a row, became heart sore and weary and spent a lot of time expressing his feelings by doing big loud smelly ones. In his last battle he and 300 of his soldiers were lucky to escape with their lives. They decided to run away, found boats and sailed to Rathlin Island.

When the people on Rathlin saw Robert the Bruce and his men coming it scared the living daylights out of them.

Bruce's men were dirty and smelly, their clothes were torn, covered in blood and sweat and they were heavily armed. The Rathlin people didn't like the look of them and ran away. Bruce chased them, caught them and said, 'I don't want to hurt you. I just want to live quietly on the island. I'll mind my own business and not do any harm.

'I want to be King of Scotland and I've been fighting the Anglo-Normans. I hate them and I've lost seven battles against them. I'm fed up! I don't think I'll ever manage to be king.' He sat down on a large rock on the shore and looked as if he could burst into tears.

The people on Rathlin felt sorry for him and said, 'You hate the Anglo-Normans? So do we. Our island is halfway between

Ireland and Scotland, so anyone who controls it controls the Irish Sea. We're sick of being invaded and bossed around by strangers. We're very happy to accept you as our king. We'll build a castle for you, feed you and be grateful if you'd flash your swords and shields at anyone who looks like invading us.'

Robert the Bruce and his merry men were happy on Rathlin. They settled down, met local girls, got married and started families. They lived there for about seven years and the ruins of their castle are still on there. Surprisingly enough, they're called Bruce's Castle.

Now this is where I get confused. There's also a cave called Bruce's Cave, which is where folklore says Robert the Bruce met a very persistent spider. The only way you can get to the cave is by sea.

I don't know why Robert the Bruce went into the cave and nobody's been able to tell me. He can't have been walking about Rathlin, suddenly needed a pee and nipped into the cave.

Folklore says Robert the Bruce went into the cave, lay back on the rough cave floor, started thinking about the many battles he'd lost with the Anglo-Normans and became very upset.

He was very uncomfortable lying on the stones in the cave, when he noticed a small spider beside him. He watched what it was doing and thought, 'That spider's like me! It has big ideas. I want to throw the Anglo-Normans out of Scotland and it wants to throw a silken thread onto the cave's roof and climb up. I keeps failing as it keeps falling down. I've failed time after time. You poor wee spider, so have you. You can't get what you want and neither can I.'

He started counting the number of times the spider tried to throw a line up to the roof. One, two, three, four, five, six, seven.

Success! The spider threw a thread up, it reached the roof and stuck firmly. The spider climbed up and looked down.

Robert the Bruce was astonished. He thought, 'That wee animal's trying to tell me something. It failed seven times. I've failed seven times. I'm like the spider, except I've given up. I mustn't do that. That spider's saying, "If at first you don't succeed try, try again.'" He took his men back to Scotland, defeated the English in 1314 at the Battle of Bannockburn and became King Robert the Bruce of Scotland.

You can be like Robert the Bruce and visit Rathlin. You can sail on a ferry from Ballycastle to the island. Today lots of people go to Rathlin because it's very beautiful and it has a famous bird sanctuary.

I get it! If at first you don't succeed, try, try again!

12

MAGGIE'S LEAP

don't know the exact date when a man called Deegan was born. All I can say is it was around 1750 and he lived on the South Down coast, near Newcastle.

In those far-off days many people were starving. Some actually starved to death. The sea and rivers were full of fish, there were lots of rabbits and hares and plenty of deer in the forests that were good to eat. The trouble was a lot of the land belonged to greedy landlords who refused to let anyone use anything on it. If they found you on their property they caught you, sent you for trial and you'd end up in jail. They hired men, called game keepers, to catch trespassers. Game keepers had guns and were allowed to shoot at people, and they didn't care if they killed them!

In the 1700s most people were farmers. They grew potatoes and oats and owned a cow. They ate potatoes and drank buttermilk. The cow ate grass in the summertime and oats during the winter. If they wanted to eat meat they took a sharp knife, cut a vein in the cow's throat and collected its blood in a bucket. The farmer's wife made a pudding by mixing it with oatmeal, salt and herbs and fried it in the pan.

Cutting a cow's throat and collecting its blood isn't good for the cow, so the farmer made sure he didn't take very much blood very often and he stuck a nail in the vein to keep it from bleeding to death. Families ate that type of 'meat' at Christmas.

Deegan had a small cottage at the side of the road with a tiny garden. It wasn't big enough to enable him to grow enough potatoes to feed a family, so he became a poacher. In other words, he stole food from the local landlords.

In those days a lot of woman died when they were having babies and Deegan's wife died when Maggie was born.

Poor Deegan was heartbroken. He didn't get married again and his wee daughter, Maggie, was the apple of his eye. When she was a baby he carried her everywhere he went. When she learnt to walk she trotted along beside him and when she grew bigger he taught her how to poach. When she was grown up she was very pretty, with long flowing hair, and she was an expert poacher.

Deegan was a good man, like Robin Hood. He stole from the rich to give to the poor. Many a poor person would have starved to death if Deegan hadn't risked his life poaching food for them.

When Deegan grew old he became weak and ill so Maggie did his job. She went poaching and managed to steal enough food to keep her friends and family alive.

One day Maggie climbed up the cliffs to the south of Newcastle and collected birds' eggs. She had a basket full of eggs when she was spotted by a troop of soldiers. She knew if they caught her with a basket of poached eggs she would be sent to jail. She was so scared she let out a big loud fart and ran away. She couldn't run towards the road because it was hiving with soldiers, so she ran towards a deep wide chasm between the cliffs near Newcastle. She was trapped. She saw huge waves breaking on the rocks below and

decided she'd rather drown in the sea or be smashed on the rocks than be caught by the soldiers. She took a deep breath, ran towards the chasm, leapt in the air, jumped over the chasm and landed safely on the other side. Not an egg in her basket was broken.

Maggie was a very clever poacher. She was never caught. She lived to be very old and died of natural causes.

Folklore says spirits of the dead often come back to earth and visit places they have loved when they were alive, and they may be thought of as ghosts. They don't do any harm, just walk around enjoying themselves. Maggie must have loved the place now known as Maggie's Leap, because her ghost can sometimes be seen there after dark, and if you're lucky you may see her repeating her famous leap.

If you want to see Maggie's Leap, go to Newcastle, on the south coast of County Down, and travel along the coast road in the direction of Kilkeel. Maggie's Leap is on the left of the road a few miles from Newcastle.

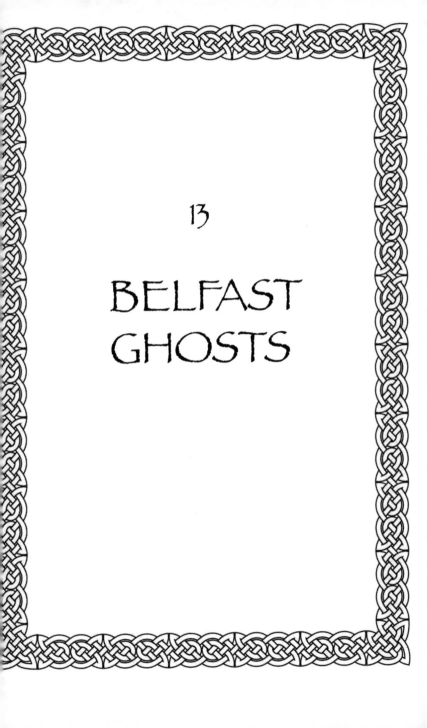

13

BELFAST GHOSTS

The Ghost of Naiose O'Haughan

Naiose O'Haughan was a highwayman who used to rob people on the roads between Carrickfergus and Belfast. He was what my granny would have called a bad egg! Many people sitting in coaches wet themselves if they heard him shout, 'Stand and deliver!' He was eventually caught and hanged on the gallows outside Carrickfergus jail. His ghost haunts the Belfast Hills.

The Sea Captain's Ghost in Skipper Street

When I was a wee girl I used to go to dancing classes held in the old Co-Op Building in York Street. It was bombed by the IRA during the Troubles, rebuilt several times and is now part of the University of Ulster, but that's another story. The point is, when I was going for a dancing lesson I used to travel by bus from the Castlereagh Road in East Belfast and get off in High Street.

There's an old narrow street, called Skipper Street, which runs from High Street towards York Street. It was a handy short cut. My mummy told me never to go there after dark because it's haunted by the ghost of a sea captain. She said, 'A pretty young woman once lived in Skipper Street. A sea captain and one of her neighbours were in love with her. One night the sea captain visited her. The neighbour was so jealous he murdered the sea captain and his ghost haunts Skipper Street.'

The Ghost in Belfast Harbour Office

Belfast Harbour Office is a beautiful building. It's near the motorway, on Corporation Street, and it's haunted by a well-dressed old man. He's never done anyone any harm. He just danders around the building or sits down for a wee snooze in a chair, but he caused a security man to nearly wet himself in the early 1990s when the harbour office was being refurbished!

During the building work many of the windows were taken out and replaced. The building was covered in scaffolding, making it very easy to break in and steal its valuable paintings and furniture, so extra security guards were hired to keep them safe.

One dark night, after everyone had left the building, the security man had been told the building was empty and he was walking along all the corridors, checking each room as he went. When he opened the door of the Moreland Room he was surprised to see an old gentleman sitting on one of the settees on the opposite side of the room. The security man didn't recognise him, so he went into the room, closed the door behind him and thought, 'I don't think I should worry. That old geezer doesn't look as if he's doing any harm. Probably he was here on business, felt tired, sat down to have a wee snooze and doesn't know the building's been closed for hours.'

He walked towards the old gentleman and said, 'Are you all right? It's very late and the building has been closed for hours.'

The old gentleman mumbled something the security guard didn't hear, walked past him, headed towards the exit and walked through the door without opening it.

The security guard's toes curled! He was so scared he telephoned Harbour Police head-quarters and said, 'Come quick! I need help. There's an intruder in the building.'

When the Harbour Police arrived they found the security man trembling with fright. He was so scared he refused to stay in the building. He left saying he was going home and he was never coming back to the harbour office!

The security man was so scared that nobody from the Harbour Police wanted to stay in the building for the rest of the night. After arguing they decided the best way to pick somebody to remain in the building was to draw straws. The policeman who drew the shortest straw nearly pooed his pants!

When the staff arrived for work the next day they found every light in the building was turned on, and a frightened policeman who was very relieved the night was over and he could go home! This appearance of the ghost was recorded in the Harbour Police incident book.

The Geraldine's Ghost

Years ago I was telling stories to a great bunch of kids in Sandy Row Community Centre, Belfast. I asked if they could tell me a story and was told about poor Geraldine, whose ghost haunts the area.

Geraldine was very beautiful. She worked in Murray's tobacco factory. She was so beautiful that one of the factory managers asked her out and she became his girlfriend.

In those days everyone was very class conscious. That means that if you were poor you could only be friends with other poor people and if you were rich your friends were rich. You knew your place and you stayed in it! It was a scandal if you crossed barriers and were friends with somebody who had more money than you.

Geraldine's friends kept saying to her, 'Be careful. Your boyfriend'll break your heart. You can't expect a well-paid mill manager like him to be serious about a poor girl who works on the factory floor.' She smiled and said, 'My boyfriend loves me. He's trustworthy. He'd never hurt me.'

Her mother said, 'Wise up Geraldine. Your boyfriend can't be serious. You mark my words. He'll ditch you and go and marry an heiress. You'll end up with a broken heart.'

One night when Geraldine came home she was so happy it would have made your glass eye water. 'Look', she said, 'My boyfriend's given me a beautiful diamond ring. He loves me and we're going to get married.'

Her mother was so upset she did a big loud smelly one. 'Geraldine,' she said, 'I told you to be careful, not to give your heart to him. Your boyfriend is having you on. He's buying you off and he'll leave you at the altar, so he will.'

Geraldine was very proud of her beautiful diamond. She insisted her boyfriend was honourable. He wouldn't lie to her. He loved her and they were going to be married.

Unfortunately disaster happened. The Germans dropped bombs on Belfast during the night of 4 May 1941. Geraldine was visiting friends on the Newtownards Road.

A bomb fell on the house she was visiting and killed everyone inside. Her body was blown to bits. Her spirit is not at rest, so you may find bits of her body haunting the area in which she moved. If you see a leg up the Lower Lisburn Road, or a head in Sandy Row or a torso lying around Murray's old factory you can bet your bottom dollar it belonged to Geraldine. The children say her hand is often seen, at night, moving across the roof of Fane Street Primary School with the beautiful ring shining in the moonlight.

Haunted John Street

There used to be a street called John Street connecting North Street and Donegall Street in Belfast's Cathedral Quarter. It's not there any more. It was demolished during the construction of Royal Avenue in the 1880s.

The ghost of an old woman haunted one of the houses in John Street. She seems to have been what my granny would have called a 'nasty auld doll' because she used to throw furniture and crockery around in one of the rooms downstairs. She was once seen walking up and down the room talking to herself and on one occasion she wrecked the back yard! She was nasty, wasn't she? But I don't think I blame her. In May 1882 some workmen found the bones of an old woman buried in the yard when they were laying new sewers and pipes. They collected the bones and buried them in the Union Graveyard and her ghost was never seen again.

I think somebody murdered the poor old soul and she was furious! I'd be furious if somebody murdered me! Wouldn't you? I don't blame her for haunting what had probably been her old home and I think it was nice of her not to haunt John Street after she'd had a proper burial. I don't think I'd have been as easily pleased! What do you think?

A Sandy Row Ghost Story

A coal porter called James Aitchison and his family went to live in number 60 Sandy Row in 1879.

The Aitchisons had a little daughter, who was 8 years of age. She slept upstairs, in a room at the back of the house. Sometimes she'd waken up in the middle of the night and start screaming. She said a strange man had come into her room, yet there was nobody there!

The Aitchison family were scared, so they moved out of the house and a labourer called Lowry moved in.

One day Lowry was up a ladder working in his back yard when he saw an old man standing at the bottom of his ladder. He called out to him and the old man disappeared before his eyes! Lowry did such a big loud smelly one he nearly blew himself off his ladder! He left the house and it lay unoccupied for years.

Scottie Shoe, the Ghost Who Haunted the Grand Central Hotel

There used to be an old, very grand hotel in Belfast, called, would you believe, the Grand Central Hotel? It was very posh, the sort of place where you didn't dare do smelly ones! It was knocked down and Castle Court Shopping Mall was built on the site. In its day it was the biggest most luxurious hotel in the whole of Ireland. All sorts of people once stayed there, like Winston Churchill, King Leopold of Belgium, Al Jolson and Billy Graham, although it was haunted by a ghost, called Scottie the Shoe.

Scottie the Shoe was a nice ghost. He didn't do anything nasty. He just walked about the Grand Central Hotel with his legs through the floor! Nobody paid much attention to him until the hotel was requisitioned by the British army. On the night of 26 May 1914 the garrison's commanding officer, William Jenkinsen, was patrolling the building when he started screaming. He was upstairs at the time. The other soldiers rushed towards him and found him lying at the foot of the stairs. He was shaking with fear. When he was asked what had happened, he said: 'I was patrolling along the top corridor when I saw a man walking towards me. He looked perfectly normal until I realised his legs were through the floor. I panicked, ran away, tripped and fell down the stairs.'

Lucifer's Match Factory Haunts Millfield Place

Lucifer's Match Factory used to be in Millfield Place. On Friday, 15 December 1882, a spark landed among the racks of matches that had been laid out to dry. As you can imagine, a spark landing among matches is not a good thing. The whole room burst into flames and the fire quickly spread throughout the factory. Four children, including the daughter of the factory manager, were employed to pack the matches. The poor wee weans (children) were trapped and burnt to death.

The factory was rebuilt and renamed simply Match Factory, and it started making matches again. People who lived near the factory were often awakened by screams coming from inside. The screaming sounds didn't stop until the factory was demolished.

14

THE WEE WOMAN FROM GLENCOLMCILLE

I love Slieve League. It's stunning and the highest cliffs in Europe are there. You can either walk or drive up near the top. I decided to walk and was very glad I did. It's a long way but it's beautiful, full of magic. Folklore says if you want to find magic, go into the west. Slieve League's on the west coast of Ireland and you couldn't get more magical than that!

There are stalls in the top car park that sell souvenirs, or drinks, or hot dogs, or lobster. I bought what must have been the best hot dog in creation. I asked the man selling them if he knew any stories about the area. He said: 'My Uncle was a great shanachie (storyteller). When we were kids he used to have us with our eyes sitting out on stalks. One of the stories he told was about the wee woman from Glencolmcille who sold strawberries.' (Glencolmcille's at the foot of Slieve League.)

'June used to be a hungry month in these parts. People ate all the food they'd managed to grow during the winter. There was nothing left to eat so the men used to catch a boat and

Ahhhhhhhhh! Yon's scary!

travel to Scotland and earn some money to keep their families from starving. There was a wee woman who lived in Glencolmcille. She used to grow strawberries, pick them, travel with the men across the sea and sell strawberries.

'One day the sea was rough. The wee woman was standing beside the rail of the boat. A big wave washed over the side, she lost her balance, was washed overboard and swallowed by a whale. The whale swam across the sea and opened its mouth wide beside the shore. The wee woman walked out and she was still selling strawberries.'

15

THE MERMAID WHO MARRIED A MORTAL

Poor Willie was very lonely after his mother died. The wee cottage they had shared on the banks of Lough Foyle seemed very empty. One day he felt all at sixes and sevens. He walked out the door, dandered along the shore and was surprised to see a girl sitting on a rock. Just looking at her cheered him up! She was combing her hair and as he watched her he fell in love. She was beautiful with long golden hair and an hour-glass figure. 'Blimey!' he whispered, 'Yon's a real wee doll. She's wheeker, stickin' out, a cracker. She's dead on!' (That's how you used to describe somebody you thought was very attractive. I think today you say, 'He or she's fit.')

The girl stood up, bent down, picked up a mermaid's tail, put it on, slithered over to the sea and swam away. Willie stood transfixed and watched until she was out of sight. He went back to his house and couldn't stop thinking about her.

Next day he decided he'd go down to the shore, hide behind a rock and see if the mermaid came back. He waited behind the rock for a long time. He was just about to give up and go home when he saw a silver streak. He watched it come closer to the shore. It was the mermaid! All the hairs on the back of his neck stood up in excitement. He watched her slither across the sand to a big rock, take off her tail and sit on the rock combing her hair. She was even more beautiful than he remembered. He decided he wanted to marry her.

Willie hadn't a baldy notion about how you go about marrying a mermaid, so he decided to visit the pishogue and asked for advice. (A pishogue was a wise woman. Every community used to have one. The pishogue knew how to use herbs and cure disease, how to help women have babies, how to lay out the dead and how to deal with fairies, witches, demons, ghosts and mermaids. Some pishogues were said to be in league with the devil.)

When Willie asked the pishogue how to marry a mermaid she said, 'Don't be crazy, Willie. You're mad to think of marrying a

She's real wee doll. She's wheeker, She's stickin' out!
She's dead on! In other words, she's fit!

mermaid. She'll go back to the sea. Forget about her and find yourself a good local girl.'

Willie said, 'I can't forget about her I love. I'd rather have a few days happiness married to my mermaid than a lifetime stuck with a local girl.'

'Well, Willie! If that's how you feel I'll tell you what to do, but mark my words – you'll live to regret it because she'll go back to the sea and break your heart.

'Go down to the shore and hide behind the rocks. The mermaid mustn't see you because you'll frighten her and she'll escape.

'When she's combing her hair, run down the shore and get her tail. That's important! If you lift her up she'll slither out of your arms, grab her tail and disappear. Pick her tail up, then lift her and carry her home. When you get home, set her down beside the fire and make her comfortable. Talk to her in a kindly fashion. Tell her you love her and want to marry her. She'll forget about the sea if she doesn't have her tail. Hide it somewhere safe. You mustn't destroy it because that would kill her. Her life's bound up in her tail and if she finds it she'll go back to the sea.'

Willie did what the pishogue suggested. He went down to the shore, hid behind the rocks and waited.

Sure enough, the mermaid came back. She took her tail off and sat looking at the sea and combing her hair.

Willie rushed down the shore, grabbed her tail, lifted her up and gently carried her home. He made her comfortable by the fire and gave her a cup of tea. She didn't like it so he went to fetch some pure fresh water from the well. When he was outside he buried her beautiful tail under straw at the back of his barn. He filled a glass with fresh water and gave it to her. She said, 'Thank you,' drank the water and sat looking round the cottage. Willie was glad he'd tidied it before going down to the shore. He'd picked his smelly socks and dirty underpants up off the floor, washed them and put them away. He'd filled the buckets beside the door full of water and dusted all the plates on the dresser so they gleamed in the firelight.

The mermaid liked his cottage. She smiled when Willie said, 'We'll have to give you a name. How about Mara?' The mermaid repeated the name several times and was pleased with it, so Willie said, 'Now we'd better go and see the minister and ask him to marry us.'

Willie and the mermaid walked hand in hand to the minister and Willie said, 'This is Mara. She's a mermaid I met on the beach and I want to marry her.'

The minister said, 'Willie I don't think the Church would allow me to marry you to a mermaid.'

Mara turned to Willie and gave him a great big kiss.

The minister blushed and stuttered, 'Hhhhere! Eeeeeasy on there! We can't have that! We can't allow any kind of canoodling between couples who aren't married.'

Mara smiled at the minister and gave Willie another great big kiss.

The minister said firmly, 'Couples who aren't married shouldn't be kissing. What will the neighbours say?'

Mara looked up, smiled and said, 'If you think the neighbours will gossip about us canoodling because we're not married, you'd be as well to marry us. I love Willie and he loves me. We won't stop kissing each other.'

The minister thought about it for a few minutes before saying, 'I think you're right. I'll marry you and I won't tell the bishop you're a mermaid. He'd be annoyed if he knew and that'd ruin my promotion prospects.'

Mara and Willie were very happy together. They had three children, two boys and a girl. Mara was a great housewife and she was very popular with the neighbours. She was always willing to give anyone a helping hand. It was Willie's fault when, years later, suddenly it all came to an end.

He used to earn a bit of extra money by making poiteen from potato skins and beetroot. (Poiteen's a type of whiskey, also called mountain dew.) Willie's poiteen was said to be delicious. (I don't believe that! I tasted poiteen once. It was vile!) Willie sold his poiteen to the neighbours and he liked a wee dram himself.

One day, Willie was making poiteen when the children spotted the revenue men, who were coming towards them. They rushed in and told Willie, who said, 'Go as fast as you can and hide the worm (part of the equipment needed to make poiteen) in the barn while I throw the poiteen in the duck pond.'

When the revenue men arrived there was no evidence to show that anyone had been making poiteen, although the ducks were staggering and flying around in a peculiar fashion because they'd drunk the pond water. You can't breathalyse a duck, so the revenue men had no proof and went away empty handed. Willie breathed a sigh of relief. You can still be sent to jail for making poiteen. It's against the law.

Willie didn't risk making more poiteen until it was coming up to Christmas. He completely forgot the mermaid's tail hidden in the barn and sent the children out to find the worm. They found the tail. It was beautiful, and what do you do if you find something beautiful? You take it to show your mummy, and that's just what they did. They rushed into the cottage shouting, 'Mummy! Mummy! Mummy! Look what we found.'

Mara was standing by the door when they burst into the cottage. She touched the tail. Her eyes changed to an ultra-marine colour, she felt the call of the sea, ran to the water's edge, put her tail on, jumped in and was never seen again.

That's not the end of the story because Mara was a very unusual mermaid. She remembered her human family and every night, after it was dark, she used to come ashore, go up to Willie's cottage and peep in through the windows. She watched Willie and her children as they slept and blew a cloud of love around them.

The mermaid's children grew up, got married and had children of their own. Each child descended from the mermaid has a little bit of webbing round their fingers and/or their toes. Look and see if you've a little bit of extra skin. If you have you're descended from

The pond's full of mountain dew!

a beautiful mermaid and you will probably be very good at swimming.

Willie grew old, died and asked to be buried near the sea. That year the spring tide rose higher than ever before. It washed away the small piece of land where Willie was buried and the locals say he's gone to live with his mermaid.

Ireland is famed throughout the world for the art of storytelling. The seancaithe and scéalaí, the tradition bearers and storytellers, passed the old stories down through the generations. Today, in the 21st century, there has been a revivial of the ancient art founded in 2003, Storytellers of Ireland / Aos Scéal Éireann is an all-Ireland voluntary organisation with charitable status.

Our aim is to promote the practice, study and knowledge of oral storytelling in Ireland through the preservation and perpetuation of traditional storytelling and the development of storytelling as a contemporary art. We aim to foster storytelling skills among all age groups, from all cultural backgrounds. We also aim to explore new contexts for storytelling in public places – in schools, community centres and libraries, in care centres and prisons, in theatres, arts centres and at festivals throughout the entire island of Ireland.

Storytelling is an intimate and interactive art. A storyteller tells from memory rather than reading from a book. A tale is not just the spoken equivalent of a literary short story. It has no set text, but is endlessly re-created in the telling. The listener is an essential part of the storytelling process. For stories to live, they need the hearts, minds and ears of listeners. Without the listener there is no story.

Le fiche bliain anuas, tá borradh agus fás tagaithe ar shean-ghairm inste scéal. Tá clú agus cáil ar na scéalta ársa agus ar an seanchas atá le fáil i nÉirinn. Le déanaí tá siad arís i mbéal an phobail, idir óg is sean, is i ngach áird is aicme.